KEN
MATTHEWS

UNFINISHED BUSINESS

BLUEPRINT PRESS
INTERNATIONALE

ISBN
978-1-961117-30-3 (Paperback)
978-1-961117-31-0 (eBook)
978-1-961117-29-7 (Hardcover)

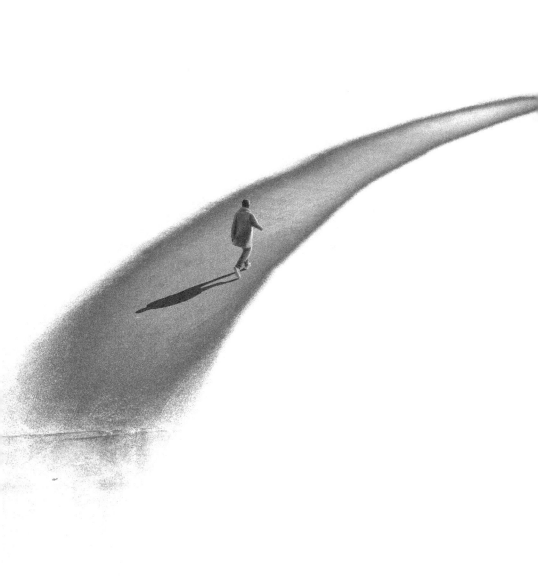

Table of Contents

Chapter One

THAT NIGHT

I t was a warm summer night in 2004 and Officer Ken Matthews is on patrol in the City of Birmingham, at the end of a long, hot shift. He is headed back to the precinct to turn in beat car 29 and then call it a night, when the dispatcher starts barking over the radio, "All units, there is a robbery in progress at Tommy's Dinner, 6975 1st Avenue, two-nine, thirty, Head that way." Officer Matthews turns on his lights and sirens and heads that way.

He responds, "Two-nine, 10-4.", then thinks to himself, "*Damn it, I just left there*", as he speeds the 5 blocks to the location.

Officer Matthews is the first to arrive on the scene. As he turns off his lights and sirens, he notifies dispatch, "Radio, 29 is on the scene, I see the suspect, hold the radio." The dispatcher replies "10-4" and the radio goes silent. The suspect is so preoccupied with robbing the diner that he doesn't see or hear Officer Matthews come through the door, with his weapon drawn. "Drop your weapon!", Officer Matthews screams at the suspect. The suspect turns and points his gun at Officer Matthews, "Fuck you. Drop your weapon bitch!" As the hammer cocks back on the .38 caliber revolver that the suspect is holding, Officer Matthews tries to keep things from going bad. He tries to talk to the suspect. "Listen! You ain't ready to die and I don't want to kill you so put the damn gun down!" A brief silence fills the air, then the suspect speaks, "man fuck you, I'ma walk out this bitch and you ain't going to do shit." Now this is not how Officer Matthews wanted this to start and it damn sure is not how he wants it to end. To Officer Matthews, it feels like time is passing slowly, at least at this moment and then...all hell breaks loose. The cook knocks over a pot, shots are fired, screams ring out and Officer Matthews is hit twice, once in the chest and once in the shoulder. The suspect is hit twice in the chest by Officer Matthews's .45 caliber service pistol. Officer Matthews is wearing his bullet-resistant vest, so the impact to his chest and the searing pain in his shoulder isn't life-threatening, the suspect, on the other hand, is not so lucky. He drops to his knees and then passes out on the floor. Blood pours out of his chest and mouth as he takes his last breath. Matthews doubles over in pain but he will live.

Matthews clicks his radio, "Two nine... shots fired...start paramedics and a supervisor...I've been shot." As Officer Matthews falls to his knees, he hears the sirens of the backup unit on its approach, then the dispatcher screaming over the radio, "Two nine backup is on the way. Two nine do you copy? Two nine do you copy? Two nine..." then lights out.

Ken wakes up from this nightmare in a puddle of sweat, looks over at the clock and it is 2:30 in the morning. IIt's been ten years since that night at Tommy's Diner and while he occasionally has dreams about it, this was the most vivid and disturbing.

He gets out of bed and walks to the bathroom, as he thinks to himself, "*That was stupid, I should have waited for back up.*" "Click" the bathroom light comes on, he looks in the mirror and there he is. Now a man in his Forties, the grey hair in his beard matches that on his head, he has just a few more wrinkles than he did last year but all in all not to bad looking.

It's almost three o'clock and I damn sure ain't going back to sleep. he thinks to himself, as he washes his face. He looks in the mirror and his mind wonders back to that night, could've done something different, could've waited for backup and coordinated a tactical entry, could've.... It doesn't matter what he thinks he could've done, that night will always be that night and nothing can every change it. *No sense in dwelling on the past. It is what it is. Might as well do my workout.* Ken thinks to himself as he leaves the bathroom and goes back into his bedroom. After his workout, he takes a quick shower and gets ready for work.

It is a beautiful morning, the sun is shining, the birds are singing, it's a cool 70 degrees and…. who are we kidding, it is 8 a.m. and not even the lukewarm coffee in his Louisiana Marines coffee cup is waking him up. As Ken is leaving his apartment, he begins to think about his day. A lot has changed in the ten years since that night…a lot. His wife of fifteen years is now an Ex, his two small sons are now two large teenagers and he is no longer a patrol officer. Now he is a Social Worker, a social worker with a very busy schedule. When he finally gets to his office and looks at his schedule, he sees that he has an appointment every hour on the hour. Yes, it is a different line of work but he is still helping the same kind of people and it is a lot of work so he settles down and gets started with the first phone call of the day. The hours seem like minutes and when Ken looks up, it's late in the morning almost time for lunch. He starts looking at his phone, trying to figure out where he is going to eat when in walks a woman from his past. A woman that he has not seen in nearly eight years. "Smiley?" she calls out.

"That's a name I haven't in years." Smiley is the nick name that the people on his beat use call him.

"Smiley, is that you?" the woman standing at the doorway asks. It takes him a minute to recognize her, but when he does, "Traniece Harolds, is that you?" in a heartbeat, Ken is on his feet, around his desk and the two embrace like old friends do, "how have you been?", he asks her and she tells him that she has been clean for the last six years and that she had started college. They look at each other for a moment and travel back to the last time that they had seen each other. Traniece use to be a prostitute on Ken's beat and from time to time, she would be his ear on the street. Every now and then if he needed a little information, she would give it to him, and in return, he would buy her something to eat. Not your everyday working relationship between a cop and a prostitute but it worked for them.

"What brings you to my office today?" Ken ask Traniece, "I am needing some help bad, I got this lil girl that is my heart, my aunt and uncle got custody and I'm trying to get her back, but I can't do that because of where I live, I need some help to make it right. "Can you help me?" Ken looks at Traniece as she takes a breath. "Where are you living?" Ken asks, "Over there, half a block up from 69th on 1st Ave." Ken just looks at Traniece and sits down into his chair but doesn't say a word. Ken can see it in her eyes that she wasn't expecting his reaction and that she senses something is not right with him but she needs his help and she asks, "Smiley, will you be able to help me?" Her question brings him back in to where he is, with hesitation he agrees to help her.

He sighs, "Let me see what I can do, give me your information and I will get back to you." When he agrees to help, she smiles, offers a final thank you and walks out of the office. Ken leans back in his chair, closes his eyes and thinks, *Damn. It started out an ok day, then she walked in…* and now, all he can think about is that night

Later that day, Ken is driving through the area where Traniece lives and what was once his beat. Nothing much has changed in the 6900 block of 1st Ave… well maybe a few things. There is a coffee shop where the adult book store use to be, the barber shop that use to be "Eddie Brother's Style Shop" is now "Tim's Cuts and Extensions" and "Tommy's Diner", well, it's just gone. It closed shortly after the shooting that night and because it was a crime scene involving an officer, it just stayed that way. On the corner where the diner was, is now a vacant building and as luck would have it, standing in front of that building next to the street light, is a man that Ken thinks he recognizes but it has been a long time. Ken stops his late model pickup, gets out and starts to walk towards the man, "Hey, how you doing this evening?" The man just looks at Ken, "Listen, I have a few questions if you have the time?", still nothing, "Do you know a woman named Traniece Harolds? She lives in the area." It takes a little time but finally he speaks, "Neicey? Yeah I know her…What you want with her?" Ken begins to speak but notices a look on the man's face, a look that he knows all too well. "I am asking about her because she asked me to help her out with a few things, I'm…" and before Ken can finish his statement, the man takes off running and Ken, without hesitation, chases after him.

One block, two blocks, coming up on the third, Ken thinks to himself, *this joker can run,* and he's having a hard time keeping up with him but then, the man trips and tumbles over into some trash cans. Ken finally catches up to him and in a slightly out of breath, obviously pissed tone ask, "why the hell did you run?" The man looks up at Ken, breathing hard from the exercise and says, "Cause you a cop." Ken looks at the man, still breathing hard and remembers the last time that he saw him, it was last time that he arrested this man. "Malcom?" Malcom Davis, was a small-time thief with a sorted history, that was always good for information, when he wasn't running from Ken, back in the day "yeah Smiley…it's me…I have been clean and straight since the last time you put me in jail…I thought you had retired?" Ken looks at Malcom, shakes his head, offers him his hand, "Let me help you up." Malcom takes the offer, rises and Ken begins to speak, "I am retired, I work for Social Services now and I am just trying to help out an old friend." Ken and Malcom sit down on one of the sidewalk benches and start to talk about how bad the area has become and how the people need someone to help them clean up their neighborhood. Unknown to the two men, while they are talking, they are being watched from the corner, half a block away. The person watching the two men is another person from Ken's past, but one that he wouldn't know. After all, they only met once but there is no way that Ken would know that. The young man watching Ken and Malcom focuses on Ken as he thinks to himself, *"You back huh bitch, yeah I'm a see you again."* He then turns and walks away. Ken gets that old spooky feeling and turns around to see what it is that is making his cop sense tingle but by the time he turns around, it is already gone.

Ken doesn't see anything but he can't shake the feeling that he was being watched. He turns back to Malcom and they finish their conversation. The two men shake hands and go their separate ways.

It's the end of a long work day and he has done all that he can do for Neicey tonight. Ken stops at his favorite restaurant to grab a bite. He sits down at the bar, his usual spot and looks at the menu. The bartender walks over, "what will it be tonight gorgeous?" Ken looks up, "Hey beautiful, I'll have the usual." She smiles and walks away, Ken starts going over everything that has happened that day, the meeting with Traniece, chasing down Malcom and that spooky feeling that he got, all these thoughts bring him back to that night. The bartender gives Ken his order to go, "Here you go doll", Ken takes the bag, smiles and thanks her. The entire drive home, Ken can't seem to get over that spooky feeling that he got when he was talking to Malcom. Something just keeps bothering him, it wasn't anything that Malcom said or did and truth is Malcom didn't have much information, just talked about how the neighborhood had changed. No, it wasn't that, Ken just could not shake that spooky feeling. *"I need a drink"* he thinks to himself as he walks through the door of his apartment. He grabs a glass and his favorite bottle of whiskey from the bar, pours a shot, takes a sip and sits back on his couch as his mind goes over the events of the day. He still cannot figure out why he had that strange feeling but it's late, he's tired, it's been a long day and he needs some sleep, so he gets up from the couch, walks into his bedroom and takes off his clothes. *"Maybe I'll figure it out in the morning,* he thinks to himself as he pulls back the covers on his bed, gets in, and turns out the lights. It has been one hell of a day, the kind of day that he hasn't had in a long time, but he made it home and at the end of the day, that's all that really counts. *I'll call Sonja in the morning, maybe she can give me some insight into what's happening on my old beat.* With that last thought, Ken is out like a light as his head settles into the pillow.

Chapter Two

AN OLD FLAME

I t's a new day but the same routine…work out, shower, breakfast, coffee, then out the door and on the road to work. When Ken gets to his office building he takes a few minutes to compose himself before he makes the dreaded but necessary call.

What?", she answers. "Hey LT it's Ken Matthews. How've you been?" The silence on the phone is deafening, then she speaks, "I know who it is Matthews…what do you want?" Despite the hostility in her voice, there was a time, back in the day, before that night, when she had his back and he had hers. After that night and his divorce, the two of them became more than Patrol Sergeant and Officer. Then for a brief time, they shared something that was both wonderful and toxic. When it was over, it was clear to both of them that some things are better left unexplored, yet somehow they were able to remain on speaking terms. At least that's what he thought, but her demeanor over the phone makes Ken pauses for a moment, and reassess his approach. He decides that the best way to get the information that he is looking for is to just come out and ask for it.

"Sonja, I need to get some information about the 6900 to the 7200 blocks of 1st Ave. What can you tell me?" It only takes her a second to respond and what she says, is not good.

"The 6900 block to the 7200 block of 1st Ave, is nothing but trouble. During the day it's all seemingly legit businesses with the illegal stuff going on in the back. At night, all the dirt comes out.

As she speaks, the sound of her voice brings him back to the time when the only thing between them was the night air and their clothes, but only for a second…if that long. She brings him back to reality just as fast as he as he fell into his fantasy world.

"Why are you asking? What are you thinking about doing? You do know that you are not a police officer anymore?" He laughs at her question, but the truth is, he has no idea of what he is getting himself into, but Neicey did ask for his help, "I know that I'm not a police officer anymore, thanks for the update. However, to answer your question, I was asking because an old friend asked me asked if I could help her get custody of her daughter and I was just trying to get an idea

of what I might be dealing with. So thank you for the info and I will be sure to remember that I am no longer a Police Officer." He tells her in the smart-ass way that only he can.

There is a moment of silence before she speaks, "Well, as long as you know that you can't do any of the stuff that you use to do and that means if you break the law, yo ass is going to jail."

Ken just smiles, "I know, and seriously, thank you. It was good to talk to you again, I haven't been chastised in a while", Ken jokes at her statement. She smirks "bye Matthews" and hangs up. *At least I have a better idea of what I'm getting myself into…I think he thinks to himself as he turns off his truck and gets ready to go into the building.*

Later that day, after a few appointments, Ken decides that if he is going to help Neicey out, he is going to need a little more information about the problem in the 6900 block of 1st Ave, so he heads back to the area to do a little investigation. He goes door to door, knocking and talking. Some people talk to him some don't, no different than when he was a cop, but those that do talk give him plenty of information. It seems that the cause of a lot of problems in the area is one man. Someone new to the neighborhood, for what appears to be the last 2 years and word is that he has his hand in everything that is going on in the three block radius. Ken finds out from some of the neighbors, that would talk to him, that they call him G and depending who you ask, he is the Devil himself.

Ken continues with his knocking and talking until he notices a car, that has been following him for the last three or four blocks. It's an old Chevy Caprice Classic, with blacked-out tinted windows. It looks like an old police cruiser that the local drug dealers like to use. He noticed it because every time he stopped; the car stopped. This continues for a few more steps until Ken finally has enough and decides to find out who's driving it and why he is following him. As he begins to approach the vehicle, it speeds off almost hitting another one coming up the road. Ken makes a mental note of the tag, pulls out his phone, and makes a call to 911, "Yeah, there's a suspicious vehicle in the 7100 block of 1st Ave, if you have unit in the area, can you start them this way?"

Ken hangs up and within 5 minutes the beat car pulls up. As the beat officer exits his vehicle and approaches Ken, he asks, "Did you call about a suspicious vehicle?" Ken approaches the officer and introduces himself. "Yeah, my name is Ken Matthews, I'm a Social Worker with the county and I was just in the area talking to some of the people in the neighborhood, trying to get some information for a client of mine, when I noticed a green, blacked out Chevy Caprice following me, when I walked up to it to see who it was they sped off almost hitting another car."

The officer just looks at Ken and that look says it all. Ken takes a deep breath, "Yeah, I know that was stupid." The officer agrees but has no information to give Ken about the car or this G that everybody is telling him about. The officer gets into his car and tells Ken that he will keep an eye out for the blacked-out Caprice and drives off. Ken figures that it would be best if he calls it a night, walks the two blocks back to his truck, gets in and goes home.

As Ken gets on the interstate and begins the 30-minute ride back to his apartment, his phone starts ringing, Sonja's number shows on the screen, *Awe damn. What does she want?* Ken answers his phone "Hey LT h…", she stops him mid-sentence

"I thought I told you not to be out there acting like you are still a police officer? Do you know that you could've got your ass killed? What the hell are you thinking?" Clearly she is mad at him.

"Ok listen, I was only asking around trying to find out what is going on in the area so that I can help out Traniece Harolds, you remember her, anyway she came into my office the other day asking for help to get custody of her daughter and I am just trying to find out if the area is safe for her to raise a child."

Silence over the phone, "Still, that was still stupid. Walking up to a blacked-out car, I should hit you in your head." Ken smirks under his breath, "so you're worried about me?" He asks her and she tells him, "Just don't do anything else stupid…please?" He replies, "You know me." She comes back with, "Yes I do know you and that's why I said don't do anything else stupid.", Ken smiles and decides to do one more stupid thing.

"So…what do you have planned for tonight?" he asks, and she responds with a light-hearted snicker "Good night Matthews." and then hangs up.

On his way to his apartment, he decides that that is not where he wants to be. He takes the next exit off the interstate, gets back on, and heads in the opposite direction. He makes his way to his favorite hangout, Jazz on 28th. He pulls into the parking lot and can hear live jazz emanating from the club. He parks his truck, walks into the club, pays the entrance fee, heads towards the bar, and takes a seat. The bartender walks over and asks him, "the usual?" He responds, "of course." This bartender that knows his order so well is named Mac. She and Ken go back to when he was a bouncer at another club and she was just starting out as a bartender. She brings Ken his usual, a whiskey with two ice cubes, and three fingers high. As Ken settles in and begins to enjoy the music, and takes a sip of his drink as he turns to face the band. At that moment a statuesque beauty walks in the door and stops. She stands 5'7" … 5'11" in 4" heels with a beautiful brown complexion, short pixie cut hair, wearing a fitted black dress that stops just above her knee. Full beautiful lips with red lip stick and a body that says "you must be this tall to ride this ride. Ken can't help but to be memorized by her beauty.

She walks over to Ken and speaks, "How did I know that you were going to be here?"

Ken stands to great her, as a man should for a woman that is this exquisite, "Well, seeing that this is my favorite jazz club, then add to that the fact that you and I have been here on several different occasions, it was safe to assume that I would be here, especially after a day like today" She looks at him to signal that she thinks he is a smart ass but she can't deny that he is right…this time.

He continues with a certain smugness, "And since you're wearing that, I can only assume that you were hoping that I'd be here." She tilts her head down, looks up at him and rolls her eyes, and with a slight smile on her face says: "This is what I wore to work and after the stupid shit you pulled today, I needed a drink." She tells him in her most sarcastic tone.

Ken turns and pulls out the stool next to him, motions to the bartender and orders Sonja's favorite drink. When it arrives, holds his glass for a toast and says, "You are beautiful." She agrees to the toast, clink's her glass to his and smiles.

After a drink or two or more…they lost count… the music begins to fill not only the room but their souls, he takes her hand, leads her to the floor and they start to dance. They begin to move their hips to the music as he wraps his arm around her waist and she takes his lead hand. Their hips slowly match the rhythm of the music and it isn't long before they are doing what looks like making love on the dance floor, they move as if they never left each other. She melts into him; he completely covers her. Who knows where this is going? Could this be headed to a time when they were more than just two people on the dance floor, or could this be one of those times that two people, that have been through some shit, need each other to help release the tension, the sexual tension that exists between them? Neither of them knows yet both are willing to find out. Sonja breathes in the scent of his cologne and loses herself in his embrace as Ken feels her body surrender slightly as the music continues. Their bodies begin to meld, two into one, hips to hips, breast to chest, lips to lips. Both hearts are pounding and neither can catch their breath as their tongues intertwine and each begins to breath for the other. With his arms wrapped around her body and her body pressed firmly against his, the music beats through their skin and down to their bones as they get lost in each other, the way they have many times before, then the music stops and they are back to reality. In an attempt to save the moment. He takes her by the hand and leads out of the club.

"We can't do this," she says as he leads her back to the bar. As he grabs their things, Ken turns towards her and asks, "Do what?

I'm just getting our stuff so I can walk you to your car." He says with a little bit of sarcasm in his voice as they turn to exit the club. He was hoping that their dance had meant more than it did but clearly, she didn't see it that way, or maybe she did? "Oh," she says with the sound of disappointment in her voice. Maybe she wanted him to convince her that their being together again was the right thing...at least for the night. When they make it to her car, he opens the door for her and gets

in. Ken bends down and kisses her deeply and passionately. "Thanks for the dance; I had almost forgotten how well we move together." He says with a smile on his face.

She smiles back, "you know you're not a cop anymore?" she says, and he chuckles. "I know, now drive safe and have a good night." Ken tells her as he turns to walk away.

As Ken gets in his truck, several thoughts go through his mind... those lips, those thighs, that ass, that blacked out Caprice. For some strange reason that damn car pops back into his head. Something about it felt strange but also familiar. Ken hasn't had the feelings like this in years but it's late, he is headed home...alone. When he gets into his apartment, it occurs o him that, that blacked-out Caprice could have something to do with what he is trying to help Neicey with and it scares him. He takes out his phone and calls her... her phone just rings, and he starts to get worried. He is about to hang up, grab his old service weapon from the closet where he keeps it and drive over to her apartment when she answers the phone.

"Smiley, why are you calling me this late? Is something wrong?" He is relieved to hear her voice, "Hey Neicey...no there's nothing wrong." She's not buying it and she lets him know it, but he can't let her know that something spooked him because it will frighten her. "You sound like you were sleeping, I apologize for waking you up, go back to sleep and I will talk to you tomorrow." She says ok and hangs up the phone, then he gets ready for bed. He tries to shake that feeling he keeps getting but it's not happening. It takes a few minutes, but it is 2:34 a.m. and Ken has no choice but to finally passes out from exhaustion.

Chapter Three

SOMETHING FAMILIAR

The next morning, after some coffee and a few phone appointments, Ken calls Neicey again. He needs to ask her about G and find out what is actually happening on his old beat, especially since he can't shake that old spooky feeling.

Neicey's phone rings and when she answers, she appears to be in a good mood but is curious about their last conversation, "Hey Smiley...why did you call me so late last night?"

Ken takes a minute before he asks her the question that is going to determine if he can help her, "I talked to some of the people in the neighborhood and they all kept bringing up the same name...Who is G?"

Neicey drops the phone and Ken can hear her scramble to pick it up. When she does, it's not helpful. "G?" Ken can tell from the shock voice and the way she asks her question that she knows something about this G, but that she's afraid to give him the answer. However, she does answer and what she tells him is not the answer he is not the answer that he is looking for, especially from the person who at one point in time, he got most of his information about what was going on in the neighborhood from.

"G is nobody. Just some young thug that thinks he runs things around here…." After her initial response, Neicey rambles on about everything but G. Ken decides that it would be best if he didn't push the issue, at least not on the phone.

"So, you can't tell me anything, other than 'he's a young thug'?" Neicey goes silent, "Ok, I have a meeting today, but I want you to meet with me later and I want you to tell me everything that you know about him, understand?"

Neicey sighs, "Ok Smiley, Ok." Then she hangs up the phone. Ken leans back in his chair, *You are not a cop anymore, just get the information and give it to Sonja. You are not a cop anymore.* This thought goes through his head repeatedly but it's just that, a thought, and like always he ignores his head and listens to his hear

After Ken's meeting, he makes a call to Sonja. He has no idea what her mood will be after last night but this is a call that he needs to make. She answers the phone, "Hello?" Her tone is pleasant, Ken sees his chance, "Hey LT…I need a favor? Can you get me as much information as possible about a guy named G?" A few seconds past before she answers, "I thought I told you that you are not a cop anymore and that if you go out there and do anything stupid, your but was going to get arrested?"

Her pleasant mood went out the window and Ken wasn't sure what to say next but still he asked, "Will you do the favor or won't you?" Ken has no idea why he asked her like that but he is kind of glad he did. Her whole demeanor changes and she tells Ken that she will do whatever she can. Ken's is not sure if that is a good thing or if she will make him pay for it later, either way he is grateful for her help and he thanks her, "Just be careful Matthews", is the last thing she says before she hangs up.

Ken's next call is to Neicey, he tells her to meet him at Avery's Place, A new restaurants on 1st Ave and to be there in 45 minutes. She reluctantly agrees and then hangs up; Ken gets in his truck and is headed that way.

Ken arrives early at Avery's, parks his truck, and walks towards the door. totally oblivious to the fact that he is being watched. Two blocks away from the restaurant, that blacked-out Caprice Classic is backed into an alley and it has been following him since he got into the area. The driver of the Caprice is one of G's boys named Dee and he has been keeping tabs on Ken ever since he started going door to door, talking to people in the neighborhood, trying to get as much information about him as possible, for G.

Back at Avery's, Ken sits down at a table and grabs a menu. Neicey walks in shortly after Ken orders and sits down next to him. "Hey Smiley, how is your day going?" Neicey asks, but Ken has more on his mind than being cordial, so he gets straight to the point. "Tell me what you know about G?"

Neicey shifts in her seat but she answers his question, "G is a new wanna be gangster that just moved over here a lil while ago. Nobody knows where he came from, only that he's made some major plays making some of the people that use to be dealers either move away or just go missing."

Ken listens to her every word like he did when she was his confidential informant. Neicey is still giving him everything she knows about G when he stops her, "Wait. What's G's real name?" She stops and takes a deep breath before she speaks, "I don't know his real name, all I know is G."

Ken can tell by her body langue and the look on her face that she is giving him all of the information that she has and decides that pushing her any harder will only cause her to shut down and he needs her to stay with him while he figures this all out. But the more uncomfortable she gets, the more intense that spooky feeling gets.

His uneasiness must have been showing and Neicey noticed. "What's wrong Smiley?' she asks. "Nothing, it's just a feeling." He tells her. At that moment Ken's phone rings, it is Sonja and she might have the information that he asked for.

"Neicey this is a call I have to take; I'll be right back." She agrees then Ken gets up and walks out of the restaurant to take the call. "Hey LT. What you got for me?" What Ken hears is far more than what he expected.

Sonja starts, "G's real name is Gerard Simmons and he moved back to town after his stay in prison. He was arrested for driving and wrecking a stolen car and then later confessed to being the driver for his brother who was killed in an attempted robbery back in 2004."

Ken, stops her and then asks, "What was the brother's name?" What she says next knocks the wind out of Ken, "The brother's name was David Simmons." It takes him a minute to deal with what he just heard but he recoups and Sonja keeps going, "he was then sentenced to four years in Juvenile Detention and upon turning eighteen, his sentence was commuted for five more years to the Alabama Correctional Prison…" Ken lets her finish and then thanks her for her help. In the back of his mind he can't help but to think, *What did Neicey get me into? What am I getting myself into?*

Just as Ken hangs up with Sonja he notices that same blacked-out Caprice Classic that's been following him around the neighborhood, half a block down and across the street from the restaurant. Standing next to it is the dark figure of a man. Ken starts to walk towards the figure and the figure starts walking towards him. They meet in the middle of the street, "G?" Ken asks the man. The man replies, "Officer Matthews." Both men stand there and size each other up.

Ken starts off the conversation, "I haven't been officer Matthews in 10 years, now I am a social worker trying to help out an old friend. What about you?" The way he presented the question and his posturing are reminiscent of when Ken was Officer Matthews or Smiley.

"I'm just trying to do my thing" G tells Ken and then he asks a question, "Since you ain't a cop no mo, why you trying to get in my business?" This just went from a friendly conversation to a showdown in the middle of the street.

Ken tenses up and gets ready for the fight that he knows is coming, "I'm not in your business, I'm just trying to make sure that a mother and her little girl can live together and not have to worry about some piss ant wanna be kingpin making the area where they live into something worse than a war zone."

The two men lock eyes and both refuse to back down and what seems like an eternity passes by before G speaks, "You just betta watch yourself old man, these my streets now and I'm a better shot than my brother was." Then he turns and walks away. Ken watches as he gets back into the car and it drives off.

Ken goes back inside the restaurant to confront Neicey. He walks over to her and begins to speak, "Neicey, do you have any idea of what we are dealing with? I gotta get you out of this neighborhood, so you can get your daughter back and she can grow up safe from all this bullshit."

Neicey looks at him with awe and disbelief, "Out of this neighborhood? Smiley, have you lost yo mind? I can't leave this neighborhood." She begins to plead her case and explain why she can't, no, refuses to leave.

"Not only is it hard to find a place to live that I can afford but I grew up here. These are my peeps." Ken looks at her and he can see all of the emotional pain that she would be in if she had to move. "I know that it would be difficult at first but you have to think about what would be best for you, for your daughter."

Neicey just looks at him then says, "I thought I was, that's why I came to you."

What she says puts Ken at a loss for words. What she wanted, what she needed was for Ken to be the person that he swore he would never be again. She needs Smiley.

"I am not asking for your help as a social worker Smiley...I'm asking for your help as Officer Matthews.... I'm asking the man that kept this neighborhood straight with no fear," Neicey places her hand on his chest, just over his heart, "Can he help me?" Ken can't believe that he is even thinking about giving her the help that she is asking for...but he is.

"I cannot do what you are asking me to do. I haven't been that man in years, that's why I am what I am now." The look of disappointment on her face cuts Ken at his soul.

"I thought you could help me out, but I guess I was wrong." Ken can tell just how much she needs his help, but he can't.

"I'm sorry, I'm just not that man anymore." Neicey looks at him in disbelief, she screams, "Fine, I guess I will have to do it myself." Then she turns and walks out of the door.

Ken is torn as a battle rages inside of him, a battle between who he is and who he was. He is no longer that man that the people counted on to keep them safe. That was a different time, he was a different person, but then...Bang, bang, bang, bang shots from outside and they are close. Ken gives a command to the restaurant staff, "Call 911!" as he runs out of the restaurant to find out what has happened. When he makes it outside, he sees Neicey lying on the ground bleeding. He kneels next to her and tries to stop the blood from pouring out of her like water from a faucet but it's not working. While he is doing everything in his power to stop the bleeding, out of the corner of his eye he sees the blacked-out Caprice speeding away from the scene. He looks down at Neicey and applies more pressure to her wounds.

"Smiley, they shot me Smiley, I don't want to die, not now, not before I see my little girl again." Ken looks at Neicey and tells her, "You're not going to die, I got you."

The sirens, off in the distance, are getting closer. Ken keeps applying pressure to her wound but it keeps bleeding. Neicey keeps telling him that she doesn't want to die, and he keeps telling her that she won't, but the truth is, he doesn't know, and it doesn't look good. As the sirens get closer, Neicey loses consciousness and Ken does everything that he can to keep her with him. The paramedics finally make it to them and Ken is more than willing to let them take over. Ken backs out of the way so that they can work. While the paramedics are working to save Neicey's life, the police arrive and begin to question Ken. Ken gives him all of the information that he has as the paramedics load Neicey into the back of the ambulance, then race off to the hospital, lights flashing, sirens screaming. Ken neglects to tell the officer about the blacked-out Caprice Classic that he saw speeding from the scene or about the conversation that he and G had.

"Is that all you can tell me?" The officer asks Ken. "Yeah that's all that I know…I heard the shots, came outside and found her on the ground." Ken looks at the officer and he can tell that the officer thinks that there is something Ken isn't telling him, but the officer doesn't push the issue. He looks at Ken and tells him that they will be in touch and that he should probably go home. Ken thanks the officer and watches as he gets in his car and drives away. When Ken makes it back to his truck, he stops and just looks at his blood covered hands. He tries to make sense of what just happened and piece together the events of the night and how he could have kept them from happening but he realizes that he couldn't have done anything to prevent the nights' events. As he gets into his truck, he can't help thinking about the look on Neicey's face when he told her that he couldn't do the one thing that she came to him for, to help her but now the blood on his hands has given him a new prospective. Now he's pissed.

Chapter Four

REMEMBER THE TIME WHEN...

Ken has been in the shower now for more than an hour, trying to clear the night's events from his mind, the way he did with the blood that covered his hands, with hot water, soap, and steam, but it's not working.

He keeps telling himself that what happened was out of his control... that's what he keeps telling himself, but he doesn't believe it. He is thinking that had never gone back to his old beat, had he never started asking questions, had he never.... the list could go on, but the fact remains that he did and now he has to figure out a way to fix it.

As he steps out of the shower and grabs his towel to dry off, he hears someone banging on his apartment door and screaming his name. Ken wraps his towel around his waist, walks into his living room towards the door and grabs his gun from the hall closet and asks who is it. "Open the damn door Matthews!"

It's Sonja and she sounds pissed. Ken reluctantly opens the door, "What the hell did I tell you? I thought I told you that if you got in trouble that your ass was going to go to jail. What the hell were you thinking? You weren't thinking. You know that could've been you?"

Ken slowly raises his hand like a kid in elementary school and she pauses, "Do you want me to answer any of those questions or do you know all the answers?" he asks in the smart ass, slightly pissed off way that he does when he is trying his hardest to ease the tension without cussing someone out.

She stops and just looks at him, even more pissed than when she got to his apartment "Don't try me Matthews.", she says. Ken looks at her and he begins to explain that he was trying to avoid everything that happened.

"I'd just told Neicey that I was not going to be able to help her and that I thought she should move out of that neighborhood. Then she stormed out of the restaurant and the next thing I know, shots were fired and when I made it outside, I found her on the ground, bleeding.

Sonja can't stop being pissed at him for not listening to her instructions and for putting himself in harm's way but being that she knows this man, both professionally and intimately, it doesn't take long for her anger to subside once she sees that he is ok. She reaches out, puts her hand on the side of his face and steps in closer to him. "I'm sorry; it's just that when I heard what happened, it scared me. You're not a cop anymore and I need you to understand that." Ken looks her in her eyes and mumbles, "I know."

She then steps in closer as old feelings begin to come alive in the both of them. He puts his arms around her waist and pulls her into him. With a small gasp, she surrenders to his embrace. Their lips meet as their tongues begin to dance. They share each other's breath as it is going to be their last. It doesn't take long for them to fall back in to the feelings that the once shared for each other. Ken's hands move from the small of her back to the curved, soft mound of flesh that is her derriere. He grabs hold as if it was still his. She begins to protest but gives in completely and she settles into his hands. Her fingers trace every inch of his sculpted arms, shoulders, chest and back. His hands roam over every inch of her body that he can make his. From her soft supple rear to the back of her neck where he takes control of this moment. Her hands stroke the back of his neck down to his shoulders as she digs her fingernails into his skin, reminding him that he is not the only one in this moment. He reaches down and grabs her by her thighs, then lifts her feet off the floor as she wraps her arms around his neck and her legs around his waist causing his towel to come loose and fall to the floor. She holds on to him as if her life depended on it and prepares herself for the passion that is about to fill her. He carries her to the couch in the living room, because it is the closest flat surface with cushioning near them and he does not want to chance losing the mood. He lays her on the couch and stands before her in his full glory. Sonja takes a minute and admires every inch of his chiseled frame but can't help but to focus on the increasing presence of his maleness. He watches her breast rise and settle as the speed of her breathing increases. He lies on top of her and She feels the weight of his body as it covers her. They kiss, as he slowly begins to unbutton her blouse and then pulls it out of her skirt. He kisses down her neck, to the top of her cleavage and she removes her bra, allowing her breast to be tantalized by his lips. He kisses his way down to the top of her skirt, "this will have to go" he tells her and with one tug, removes her skirt and underwear. Now, she is laying there in nothing but her peep toe pumps. She off her shoes, then Ken resumes kissing her at her naval and slowly makes his way to the crease where her thigh and hip meet, then to the inside of her thighs and up to that spot that can only be described heaven, where his tongue swirls around her sweet spot. She gasps, arches her back and grabs at whatever she can get her hands on, "OH FUCK!" she screams as he brings her to the edge of pure bliss. She has the first of the many climaxes that the night will bring, and just before she reaches her next, he stops and moves into position. He lines himself up with the opening of her sex and slides in with one thrust, filling every bit of what makes her a woman. Her hands slide down his back and firmly grasp his ass, as he makes his home inside of her. She wraps her legs around his back as he begins to slowly move in and out of her, over and over and over. Their lips embrace and their tongues intertwine as the passion increases and their bodies become one. He grows in her and she melts all around him. The closer he gets the more she encourages him to bring her to pure ecstasy. It's not long before he explodes deep inside of her and she embraces him completely as he collapses on top of her but the night is not over, not by a longshot. He lifts himself off of her and brings her with him. He sits back on the couch and she straddles him. Her breast are in full view, he has no choice but to take one and make it his own. She holds his head against her as he attempts to take her full breast into his mouth. He takes control of her ass as he lifts her up and then lowers her onto his fully erect manhood. All she can do is accept him into her as she slides onto him. She begins to ride him as if he were a bucking bronco, pressing his head hard into her breast. He takes a firmer hold of her ass and sucks her full breast into his mouth. It's not long before she is coming to another climax, it builds from deep inside of her, Ken feels it rise in her and he prepares himself for the explosion that will follow. She erupts in a climax like nothing she has ever experienced and Ken, well he is just along for the ride. She collapses onto him and lays there but only for a second. Ken is too close to what he has been building to stop and let her catch her breath. He stands with her still on him, turns her around, puts her on the couch on her hands and knees and then slides deep into her with one thrust. Now, he is in charge and he is taking full advantage. He slides in and out of her with strong, powerful thrust and all she can do is hold onto the back of the couch for dear life and scream, "Oh Fuck!" with every stroke. His hips relentlessly slam into her ass and with each stroke he goes deeper and deeper into her sex, bringing himself closer to the climax that he has been working for. Each stroke has her on the edge of sheer bliss as she saviors each and every one. Over and over and over again, all the way in and then almost completely out, each stroke stronger and harder than the last, until finally they both explode in pure ecstasy. He, deep inside of her and she all over him. He collapses on her back, totally drained of everything that had been building deep inside of him and it takes all that she has to support both her weight and his on the back of the couch. Totally spent, he kisses her on her neck and shoulders, then rolls over and takes a seat on the couch. She comes down and sits next to him. He falls over to the arm rest and she falls over onto his chest. They lay there, trying to catch their breath. Before long, they are both asleep, Ken with his head on the arm rest, Sonja with her head on his chest. It is a warm night so there is no need for covers. They fall off to sleep, embraced in each other's arms, not knowing if this is a onetime thing or the start of something new but they can figure it out in the morning over breakfast, for now they will just enjoy the after effects of what just happened.

◆   ◆   ◆

The sun is rising, it's the next day and Sonja wakes up on Ken's chest. Her moving wakes Ken, "Good morning, did you sleep well?" he asks.

She looks at him and then speaks, "Last night did not happen, we did not do that." she tells him as she begins to scramble for her clothes.

Ken is confused and ask himself several questions, *Didn't she come to my apartment last night? Didn't she initiate everything that happened?* Ken looks at her, and then asks her, "Then why did you come over here last night?"

Sonja stops what she is doing and responds, "I came over here to tell you to leave this to the police. I came to tell you to stay out of it." Ken just looks at her with amazement in his eyes, and then ask the question; "You couldn't tell me that over the phone?"

By this time, she is fully dressed and headed towards the door, "Look Matthews, just stay out of it. If I find out you are messing around in this, I will arrest your ass myself. Do you understand?" and then she leaves, slamming the door behind her. Ken is left there on the couch, in utter confusion, trying to figure out what happened between good morning and her getting dressed. He gets up, still confused and goes to take another shower, while in the shower, he plays everything that happened, last night and this morning, repeatedly in his head. Not so much what happened with Sonja, that is what it is but what happened to Neicey, that is something that he can try to fix, and against his better judgement, that is what he is going to do.

Ken steps out of the shower, towels off, wipes the fog from the mirror and looks into his own eyes, *Can't deny it any longer, this is you, this who you are. You know what you have to do, you know how to make it right.* And just like that, as if a light switch was kicked on, Officer Matthews...Smiley is back. Ken walks into his room, gets dressed, goes to his closet, and straps his old service weapon on his hip. Ken is headed back to the neighborhood with the intention of coming up with a plan to help Neicey and possibly, find G.

Within an hour, Ken is back in the neighborhood, asking questions and looking for G. He asks a few people but no one has seen or heard from G. Then, out of the corner of his eye, Ken sees a green, blacked out Caprice and it has been following him for a couple blocks. Ken walks on a few more steps and the car is in tow. Without warning, Ken takes off running and the car speeds up to catch him. Ken runs around a corner and down an alley that appears to be a dead end. When the car turns the corner, Ken is gone. The man driving the car, G's boy Dee, stops the car, gets out and starts to look for Ken. He looks behind dumpsters, in piles of trash, he even climes a fence to see if Ken is on the other side but Ken is nowhere to be found. Dee gets back in his car, picks up his phone to call G and tell him that he lost Ken, then klick. Dee hears the hammer of Ken's Smith & Wesson .45 ACP go back and feels the muzzle of the gun pressed up against his right ear.

"Why the fuck are you following me?" Ken asks the man, from the back seat of the car. , "Oh shit, SHIT!" he screams, "I was just told to follow you, that's all he told me to do." Ken lowers the hammer on his gun,

"Tell your boy not to worry, I'll find him when I'm ready." Ken then tells him, "This is your one freebee with me, now drive away." and then exists the vehicle. Ken watches as the car pulls off, he knows, this is not going to end well but it's not anything that "Smiley" can't deal with.

Chapter Five

A PROMISE MADE

It has been almost two weeks since Neicey was shot and thankfully she survived. However, she has been in a coma since the surgery that removed one bullet from her upper chest and two bullets from her abdomen, but she is strong, and the doctors are hopeful that she will come out of it soon. Ken has called the hospital twice a day, every day, to check on Neicey but unfortunately nothing has changed with her condition.

After the shooting and the incident with Dee, Ken took a few days off to collect his thoughts and do some reflection on his actions. Ken decided that it would be better for everyone involved if he stepped back and let the police handle the problems on his old beat. Now he is back to work and the day is going as it usually does when his phone rings. It's the hospital calling to let him know that Neicey has come out of her coma and is responsive. Ken grabs his keys and is headed to his truck. In ten minutes Ken is at the hospital, he walks pass the information desk and straight to the elevator. When he gets to Neicey's room, the door is open, and her family is there with her. He stops in his tracks while he decides if it would be better for him to come back later and let them have their time with her or introduce himself and make sure she is ok but before he can make up his mind, "Smiley", Neicey calls out stopping him from turning around and walking away. Every person in the room, that is not Neicey, turns to see whom it is standing in the doorway.

Niece speaks again, "Y'all, this is officer Matthews…sorry Ken Matthews and he's the one that kept me alive…" Ken is now the center of their attention" …and he is going to help me get things right." Ken is surprised by what she says but she did just come out of a coma and Ken is not one to dash everyone's hopes, so he lets it slide. "Good morning everyone." Ken greets the room.

The personnel introductions are brief, her mother, an aunt and uncle, two sisters, and her daughter. Just as soon as everyone says hello to Ken, the uncle walks over to him.

"Officer Matthews" he says to Ken with an intense glare, "Just call me Ken…" Ken replies, "…and you are?" Neicey's uncle is an old man that looks like a young man that looks like he has been through hell and back and then back again. He looks Ken square in the eyes and says, "I'm her Uncle Tommy…" and without skipping a beat, "Do you know who shot my baby girl?" he never breaks his gaze.

Ken thinks before he answers, a little because he wants to fix this problem himself but mostly because uncle Tommy scares the hell out of him and that is not easy to do. "The police are handling, and I think it is better that we let them." "Hum", Uncle Tommy grunts but agrees, for now.

" Excuse me", Ken says as he walks past Uncle Tommy to talk to Neicey.

"Neicey, I am glad that you are ok, but I don't think that I will be able to do what it is that you want me to do and stay out of jail. I told you that I am not that man anymore and that's who you're asking for."

Just then, the little girl climes up on the bed and nuzzles into Neicey's arms, Neicey squeezes her, kisses her on her forehead and through tears, starts to speak, "Smiley, I know what you said but I know you and this ain't something you can leave alone….no matter how many times you say that you're not that man anymore. I know you."

Ken apologizes to her and tells her that he will never be that man again but that he will try to help her as he is now. She nods in acceptance, tells him ok and then he walks out of the room.

As Ken leaves her room, he can't help but consider what helping her would mean. A major issue playing havoc on his thoughts is that he does not want to go to jail and if he helps Neicey and things go wrong, that's where he could end up…at least that's what Sonja told him would happen.

Never the less, Neicey is pleading for his help and because of who he is, he is going to try. Just as Ken reaches the elevator he hears the sound of worn down cowboy boots approaching. Ken turns to see Uncle Tommy walking up to him. Before Ken can get on the elevator, Uncle Tommy stops him. "Hey, I need to talk to you." Five more steps and they are standing face to face.

"You do know who shot my baby girl, don't you?" Ken hesitates but only for a second, "I have an idea but like I told you before, we need to let the cops handle this." "We?" Uncle Tommy responds with a puzzled look on his face...." Whatcha got in mind?" he asks Ken.

Ken just looks at this hard, grizzled, crusty old man but doesn't speak. Then he notices an Eagle, Globe, and Anchor tattoo on his right forearm and it tells Ken everything he needs to know about this grizzled, skin like dried leather, old man. In that instant, Ken knows that he can trust Uncle Tommy, but he still isn't sure about doing what he is thinking about doing.

"I don't have anything in mind, like I told your niece, I am not that man anymore." Uncle Tommy knows better so he just looks at Ken and grunts "Humph, I know that look in your eyes. I've seen it way too many times in all my brothers' eyes, right before all hell breaks loose. I want you to take my number, you call me before you go do something stupid.... I might want in."

The men part ways, Ken gets on to the elevator and Uncle Tommy goes back to Neicey's room. In those few seconds a bond is formed... more like a bond is realized and it's one that may come in handy real soon.

◆　　◆　　◆

As Ken is walking back to his truck, his phone begins to ring, it's Sonja. "Hello Lieutenant, how may I be of service?", Ken asks in his smart-ass tone. "Matthews, I thought I told you to stay your ass out of this?"

Ken isn't surprised that she's pissed just that it took her so long to get that way after the last time they talked. "I was wondering when you would call." he tells her, and it pisses her off even more, "I told you to keep your ass out of police business and I find out that you are jumping in cars and pulling guns on people, telling them that you gonna handle this shit... You done lost your damn mind."

Ken pauses for a minute, "Wait, how do you know about that? It was just me and that fool in the car and he was following me not the other way around." The silence comes through the phone like a bullet through the air; Ken thinks back to the other day when the incident that she is talking about occurred and there was nothing out of place, nothing that should have caught his attention that didn't. How the hell does she know what happened? Then the thought hits him like a runaway train, *She must be having me followed.*

"Do you have someone following me?" she says nothing. "Ok, maybe I need to make somethings clear; Number one, I am a grown-ass man that can handle my own shit and I don't need you watching my every move. Two, After all, we have been through, you have the audacity to call me, scream at me like a child and tell me to stay out of something that had you and your police department been doing your job, I would have never needed to get into especially with you knowing what I am capable of."

Ken stops and catches his breath, this is a level of anger that he has not felt in a long time, a long time. Only a minute passes but Ken has calmed down enough to speak, "Sonja, if you think that having someone follow me the whole damn day is a good idea, then so be it but you better ask the chief about the proper use of personnel and resources." Ken hangs up, gets into his truck and heads back to work.

•   •   •

Once back at work, Ken finishes up with the case that he was working on before the hospital called. It's not a difficult case but after talking to Sonja, he is really not in the mood to do any work but he powers through his feelings and works on the case in front of him.

It is the end of day and it couldn't have come fast enough. The conversation with Sonja put him in a bad mood and it was all downhill from there. Thank the heavens it's quitting time and Ken could really use a drink. He leaves his office and heads to his favorite jazz club. Luckily for him, there is a live band tonight and Mac will be making the drinks strong. Ken walks through the door and the sound of the band fills his ears. This is just what he needs to help clear the day from his mind. He sees an open stool at the bar, he makes his way there, sits down and orders, "Hey Mac, Two and Three" is all Ken says. Mac puts two huge ice cubes in a glass and then pours three shots of whiskey. She hands Ken his drink, "rough day?" she asks. Ken just looks at her and nothing else need to be said.

"I'll have the next one ready when you are." She smiles and walks away; Ken closes his eyes, takes a sip and tries to let go of everything that happened after he left Neicey.

A few hours pass by, Ken is at the end of his third drink and feeling much better then when he came in. The music becomes lively and people are starting to fill the dance floor. Ken has his back to the dance floor when a hand touches his shoulder. More than a little intoxicated, Ken turns around to see who it is, and Sonja is standing there.

"I didn't have you followed. You forget, the streets have eyes and ears and they are talking up a storm about Officer Smiley threating to put G down." Ken just looks at her in disbelief. After all this time does she really think that he would just go after someone without a damn good reason? He doesn't want to be bothered with her at this moment, but he doesn't push her away.

He looks at her for a few seconds then speaks, "You know me better than that." The music begins to slow down, and people leave the dance floor. All the words that needed to be said were said and as Sonja turns to leave, Ken grabs her hand. She stops and turns; their lips meet as Ken pulls her in closer. The music fills the room as they break their kiss and Ken leads her to the dance floor. Time stops as they move into each other. It doesn't take long for their bodies to become one with the music. They get lost in the moment and almost forget where they are until the music stops bringing them both back to reality. Ken says to her, "Let's get out of here" and she agrees.

◆ ◆ ◆

The next morning, they are still in each other's arms. While he was mad at her the night before, the last few hours have given him a whole new prospective on their relationship. He kisses her on her forehead and she wakes up, he tells her good morning and she looks at him with a look on her face of, how did we get here again? Ken knows that look, he saw it on the face of his ex, just before their marriage ended and he has seen it from her on a few separate occasions.

She tells, "I need to go, we can't keep doing this." as she gets up and starts looking for her clothes. Ken watches her while she gets dressed and wonders to himself why she won't just let things happen like they do when two people are in love, but he knows that will never happen. Still, he tries to ease the tension the way that only he can.

"Hey, it's Saturday morning, maybe we could just lie in bed and talk about old times, do what we did last night?" she stops, looks at him and then finishes getting dressed. She will take partial credit for what happened the night before but she is not looking to start their romantic relationship again.

"This was not supposed to happen; I don't know why I let you talk me into this again. Where are my panties?" Ken reaches over to nightstand next to the bed and takes them off the lamp, where she threw them the night before and hands them to her and reminds her that it takes two willing participants to do what they did.

"As I recall, you were just as into what happened last night as I was and you didn't have any objection then, so why now?"

Sonja stops and looks at Ken, "you know this is not going to work out. Yes, we have chemistry, sexual chemistry, but that is not enough and never has been. Now I have to go, I know that I can't tell you what to do and I know threating you with jail time…. well that is a waste of time, just be careful and cover your ass." With that she walks out bedroom and then out of the apartment. Ken, emotionally drained from the day before, last night and 5 minutes ago, rolls over and goes back to sleep.

Ken wakes up a few hours later, gets out of bed and goes into the kitchen to get something to eat. As he stands there waiting for the coffee to finish brewing, everything that's happened over the last few weeks runs through his mind and then, like a train going full speed into a brick wall, it hits him, *I know how to get G, I know how to help Neicey, I just need some back up.* Ken searches for his phone and when he finds the number that he is searching for, he makes a call that will put his plan in motion. The phone rings, and an old familiar voice answers.

"Hello, who is this?" the voice asks Ken. "Tim, this is Ken Matthews and I need a favor?" Tim McAlister is one of Ken's old patrol buddies, now a sergeant in Ken's old prescient. They go over the problems on his old beat and talk about some of the things they use to talk about when they were on the streets. Ken ends the call with, "I will be there later today to go over the plan…. alright, thanks, later." Hangs up his phone and eats his breakfast.

Chapter Six

I REMEMBER THIS GAME

K en stands at the door, greeting the neighborhood residents as they walk into the meeting hall to discuss and develop a plan to take their neighborhood back and run G and his boys out for good. For the last two weeks Ken has been busy putting his plan into motion. He has gone door to door talking to residents, handing out flyers and letting everyone know about the meeting. The night of the meeting has arrived and the house is packed. Ken is nervous as he approaches the podium to start the discussion of how to turn the neighborhood around. When he gets to the podium, he introduce himself and all eyes are fixed on him.

"Hello everyone, my name is Ken Matthews, some of you may remember me, and I am sure that some of you don't... but the fact that all of you are here means that none of you are happy with the way things are going in this neighborhood... and that you want to make things better."

After Ken introduces himself and gives his speech a member of the crowd shouts, "We know who you are. What I want to know is why are you here? You quit and left us with this problem and now you want us to put our lives at risk because you are feeling guilty?" Silence fills the room, making seconds feel like hours, until Ken speaks breaking the silence.

"I'm sure that those of you who remember me, remember a man that wasn't afraid to kick in doors and put himself in harm's way, but that was then, and this is now. That man is gone, and I am here to talk about now. I came here tonight to help all of you make your neighborhood a better place to live, a better place to raise your children…hell, just better than what it is right now. That's why I'm here."

Once again, the room falls silent and all eyes are on Ken. From the back of the room a small, elderly female voice asks the question, "What can we do?"

Ken replies, "I am glad you asked that question, we all know what or who the main problem in this neighborhood is and we know what we need to do to fix it." The people in the room all know who Ken is talking but they are too afraid to say his name, much less stand against him.

The Voice from the back of the room speaks, "But what are we supposed to do? If one of us speaks out, he will kill us and if we kill him, we going to jail. If we call the police, he finds out and by the time they get here, he's gone and then we have to deal with him…. we better off just letting him do his thing."

Ken knows the feeling of helplessness that the people are talking about, but he also knows that if they don't fix it now, it will only get worse. "I know the situation seems hopeless, like there are no options but I am telling you, together you can make a change, together y'all can run this little shit out of the neighborhood, hell, out of the city. You just have to believe that you can, and I am here to help." Ken knows that this is a big order and that this is going to be a fight for the neighborhood, but he is ready. The question is, is the neighborhood? "Officer Matthews, how much help are we going to get from the you and the police?" the voice from the back of the room asks.

"Please, call me Ken, and I am glad you asked that question. I have been talking to one of my old buddies at the police precinct and we think that we have a solution. Any time you see something going on, call 911 and they will come. If someone tries to intimidate you, call 911 and they will come, in addition to you calling for everything you see, the police department is going to increase patrols in the area and a better relationship between the community and the police needs to be established. So when you see an officer, say hi and introduce yourself and that's how the community can develop a better with not just the police, but with your neighbors as well. Now this is Sergeant McAlester from your prescient and he is going to take it from here, Sergeant McAlester."

After he introduces his old police buddy, Ken steps aside and his friend takes center stage. While Sergeant McAlester is talking, Ken steps outside for some fresh air. The night is brisk, the sky is clear and the moon is full. Ken reaches into his coat pocket, pulls out a cigar, lights it and inhales deeply. He looks up and notices the blacked-out Caprice Classic parked across the street. He exhales and takes another drag off of the cigar, blows it out and looks back over his shoulder at the meeting, then back at the car and starts to walk towards it. As Ken to cross the street, towards the car, the door opens and out steps G and he begins to walk towards Ken. They meet in the middle of the street like two warriors prepared to do battle.

"I see you tryin ta organize these people against me? Dat shit ain't gonna work. Bitch, you know who I am? I'm G and these my streets." G exclaims as he hits himself in his chest. Ken just looks at him, takes another drag off of his cigar and blows the smoke in G's face. This pisses G off but at this point he needs to know that Ken is not scared of him.

Ken sees the anger swell up in G's eyes and then lets him know who he is, "I don't think you know who I am exactly. I am that one person that you do not want to piss off and guess what? You done did that and now, I have got to make your life a living hell and that is what I do best."

G steps back and looks at Ken. The look in his eyes puts fear in G but he shakes it off. "I know who you use to be but you ain't got the law behind you no mo!" G says with the authority of a two-year-old.

Ken takes another drag of his cigar, blows out the smoke, and asks the question, "and that means what?" then stares G down. The two men stand there, each refusing to be the one that turns and walks away first but then, one breaks. "This ain't over" G says, as he slowly backs away.

Ken stays in the middle of the street as G gets into his car and then pulls off. Ken takes another drag of his cigar, looks at it and sees that it is more than half gone, drops it to the ground and grinds it out with his boot. Ken laughs and thinks himself, *This is going self to be all kinds of fun.* then heads back to the meeting.

◆　　　◆　　　◆

As Ken drives through the neighborhood, he sees that people are out and about, talking to each other and getting rid of any signs that it was once one of worst neighborhoods in the city. It has been two weeks since the neighborhood meeting and the area is really starting to turn around. Everywhere, there are signs of change and growth. The people of the neighborhood are really coming together, and Ken couldn't be more thrilled. There is a block party planned for Saturday and the people are really looking forward to it. Ken thinks, What could be better than the neighborhood coming together and making such a huge turnaround? Then he comes up with an answer and it's a good one. Neicey will be there with her family and that makes Ken feel like he has fulfilled his promise and he couldn't be more pleased with himself...and the neighborhood... but mostly himself.

Ken stops at Neicey's apartment to check on her and her little girl. Her name is KeKe, but everybody calls her Baby Girl. He walks up the stairs to her apartment and knocks on the door. When it opens, he is greeted by the biggest smile that a three foot, two inch, thirty-seven-pound little girl can give. "Smiley", she squeals, He laughs and smiles, "Hey kiddo!"

He reaches over and he picks her up, she wraps her arms around his neck and squeezes with all her strength. "Wow, that was a good hug." He tells her as he puts her down. "Where's your momma and does she know you are letting strange men into the house?" She giggles and tells Ken, "you're not strange" and then runs of to get her mother.

Neicey comes into the living room where Ken is and greets him, she is still in pain but better than she was, "Hey Smiley", he just looks at her and then says," Ken, I told you that I am not that man anymore." She apologizes and takes a seat. They discuss how things are changing in the neighborhood and how things are looking better for her to get custody of Baby Girl. Ken is happy for the two of them and it shows but it is getting late and he has to go home and get some rest.

As he is walking out of the door Neicey stops him and asks, "if you're not doing anything Saturday night, me and Baby Girl would love it if you came to the fair with use?" Ken pauses for a minute and then says, "I would be honored" and from her mother's room, he hears Baby Girl scream, "Yayyyy!" He looks at Neicey and she tells him, "I'll tell her you said yes."

• • •

It's Saturday night and the block party is in full swing. The people from the neighborhood are all enjoying the festivities, and Neicey and Baby Girl are there with Ken. He is playing surrogate uncle to Baby Girl. There are all kinds of games and rides for the children and Baby Girl is making Ken do everything that a real uncle would do and like a real uncle, Ken is getting tired.

He tells Baby Girl, "Ok, we have tried every prize-winning game out here, I am almost out of money and you ain't hitting nothing. I thought you were good at playing these games?" He asks her, with a smile on his face. Baby Girl knows that she can get pretty much anything she wants from Ken, so she doubles down, "One more game, Pleeeaaassse?" both knowing that it will never be just one more. Ken shakes his head, "Aw hell, ok" as he reaches in his pocket for more money.

The night is going off without a hitch until a few of G's boys show up and start making their presence known. "We oucher tonight to let y'all know that we don't like what y'all trying to do round here. Now y'all need to carry y'all asses back inside so we can get back to our business!" Dee, the leader of group yells out as he walks down the block, creating a scene.

The people stop and look at the small group of thugs. It is apparent that they have been drinking and it looks like they are in the mood to show their asses. Unfortunately, there are no police officers at the block party because Ken and the organizers didn't think they would need them...they were wrong.

The young thugs continue to create a scene as they walk up the sidewalk, knocking over food tables and acting as if they are looking for a fight, until...." SMACK!" The sound of a hand going across the face of the leader resonates down the block. The little old lady with the small voice from the neighborhood meeting slaps the young fool and stops him in his tracks.

When Dee looks at who just hit him, she gives him what for, "You have the nerve to come into our neighborhood and try to scare us back inside, not no damn more! I have lived here all my life and I refuse to live afraid of you young thugs any longer. Now tell your boss get out of my neighborhood."

The crowd that has gathered around and the group of thugs are silent. Ken cannot imagine this night getting any better until he sees the leader draw back his hand to strike the old lady. As if he was the fastest man on earth, Ken runs across the street, grabs the man's wrist and his throat and pins up against the wall next to the old lady. With his feet dangling in the air, the young thug struggles as Ken push him harder into the wall

"Hold on now partner, you done lost you damn mind" Ken says to Dee as he holds him there. The small group of thugs that are with him are stopped by a few of the men from the neighborhood that were there. The young thug that Ken has against the wall, the rest of the thugs and the neighborhood people are in shock that Ken can move that fast but the shock wears off as the crowd begins to surround them.

"Nigga let me go", gurgles Dee as he tries to fight and struggles to breathe. The little old lady touches Ken on his shoulder, "Let that fool down baby, he will get what is coming to him, you can believe that." Ken looks over his shoulder and sees calmness in her eyes and it instantly cools him down.

"Tell your boy G that if you or he ever brings shit like this into this neighborhood again, y'all will all find out how I got the name Smiley." then Ken releases his grip and lets the Dee fall to the concrete.

The group that is with the young fool rush to help him up, Ken steps back and lets them. "I'm gone fuck you up nigga", Dee says to Ken, "Bring it bitch" Ken replies in true Smiley style.

Dee and his group notice the large crowd that is standing behind Ken and around them. They decided that this might not be the best time to take on the whole neighborhood.

"This ain't over nigga" Dee screams out as they walk away. Ken watches them leave and thinks to himself, *I know it's not,* just then the little old lady walks up to Ken and ask, "Are you ok baby?" Ken looks at her and smiles, then tells her he is fine and asks if she is ok, she nods and says yes. She tells Ken, "It's going to get worse before it's done. I'm glad to see that the old you is back to help us out."

Ken smiles, "I just wish I had the old me's arrest powers." Then he laughs, "I guess that I'll just have to do it the hard way." Ken sees Neicey standing off to the side holding her little girl and walks over to them. The look on Neicey's face says that she is afraid for her daughter but the look on her daughter's face isn't fear at all but still, it took Ken by surprise when she asked, "Smiley, are you going to beat that man's ass?"

Ken and Neicey both just look at her. Ken laughs, reaches for the child, she reaches back and he picks her up, "You know, I'm not that man anymore?" he asks, "You know you are…right?" she ask back. They walk back towards the game she wants to play and hopefully the rest of the night will be uneventful, hopefully.

Chapter Seven

THAT NIGHT AT THE DINER

I t is late one night in the summer of 2004, fourteen-year-old Gerrard Simmons is at home playing video games in his mom's living room when his older brother David comes in and starts screaming at him. "Come on boy let's go. We gotta do this!" then he turns around and walks out of the house. Gerrard stops playing his game, gets up and follows his brother outside. When he gets outside his brother is walking towards the passenger side of a car that he has never seen before.

Gerrard stops and ask his brother, "Where we going? Why ain't you driving?" His brother tells him to shut up and get in the car. When Gerrard gets in the car he sees that the steering column is broken but he doesn't question his brother and he starts the car with the screwdriver stuck in the ignition.

He tells his brother, "You know I don't have no licenses." his brother says, "Shut up and drive!" Gerrard puts the car in gear and drives off. It doesn't take long for them to pull into the parking lot of the hotel, directly across from Tommy's Diner and David tells Gerrard to stay there with the car running, gets out and starts waking towards the diner. Gerrard turns up the music and zones out everything. He is oblivious to what is going on inside the diner and doesn't notice the police car pull into the parking lot. He doesn't see officer Matthews enter the diner. He doesn't see the two men with their guns pointed at each other, but he does hear the gun fire.

He starts to exit the car, with the intention of rushing to his brother's aid when the second, third and fourth police cars arrive on the scene. He eases back into the car and slumps down behind the steering wheel. He watches as the officers' rush into the building, and that's all he can do is watch and hide as more police units and the Fire Department arrive on the scene. Gerrard has no idea what happened in Tommy's Diner, all he can do is stay hidden and watch as the police, fire department and then the news people swarm the parking lot of Tommy's Diner.

Gerrard watches as the Fire and Rescue crew load a stretcher with Officer Matthews into the back of an ambulance and he watches as the Evidence Technician Unit arrives and begins to cordon off the area with evidence tape and start taking pictures of the scene. He watches as the Coroner's Office arrives on the scene, goes into the building and comes out with a full body bag on a gurney and then loads it into the back of the body bus. He watches as the body bus leaves the scene and heads toward the interstate. He watches as the sun rises for the start of a new day, he watches.

As he watches, he starts thinking, *What the fuck just happened? Where is David? Who was the police they put into the ambulance?* These questions run through his fourteen-year-old mind and with no answers, he turns the car on and pulls out of the hotel parking lot. Still not knowing what exactly happened, still in shock from what he saw and heard, still with questions about what happened to his brother but with no answers and now, he must make his way home and try to explain to his mother something that he doesn't fully understand himself.

When Gerrard turns on to his street he sees two police cars parked in front of his house. He stops, backs the car up and turns towards the alley. Just as he backs up and turns towards the alley, His mother and two police officers are coming out of the house. She sees him in the stolen car and screams out his name. Gerrard stops, looks at his mother, sees the two officers and then floors it. The officers take out running for their cars, Gerrard turns and drives up the alley. The police are quickly behind him as he drives recklessly through the alley ways, tossing up dust and debris. He turns down a side alley in an attempt to lose the police cars; he looks in his rear view mirror to see if it worked. In that same moment, a truck is backing out of its driveway into the alley that Gerrard is racing down…. he never sees the truck.

◆ ◆ ◆

When Gerrard Simmons opens his eyes and starts looking around, he doesn't recognize where he is. He tries to sit up and that's when the pain kicks in. His head starts pounding and as he attempts to put his hand on his head, he begins to freak out because he can't move his arms or legs. He tries to scream but nothing comes out of his mouth and there is a sharp, stabbing pain in his right arm. The more he comes to his senses the more frightened he becomes. Totally and completely terrified, he creates such a disturbance that the officer that has been assigned to stand guard outside of his room rushes in. "Calm down boy, you gonna pull that IV out of your arm."

The officer tries to calm him down, but it doesn't work, at first. Gerrard calms down and realizes that he is in a hospital room with an IV stuck in his arm, a tube coming out his mouth, his head wrapped in a bandage, with his arms and legs strapped to the bed.

The officer calls for the doctor or a nurse to help Gerrard get the tube out of his throat and when they come in the officer steps back and lets them work.

Once the tube is out Gerrard starts asking questions, his voice barley above a whisper due the damage from the tube being in his throat, "What happened to me? How did I get here?"

The officer proceeds to tell Gerrard about the car chase that he started in the stolen car that he was driving and the driver of the truck that he sent to the hospital. The officer tells him that he is lucky nobody was killed and that because he is a juvenile he will likely be in Family Court until he turns 18 and then on state prison. All Gerrard can do is lay there and think about how got in this position and what is going to happen to him next.

◆ ◆ ◆

Almost a month has passed since Gerrard has been locked up in Juvenile Detention and he hasn't seen or heard from his mother. It is the day of the day trial and Gerrard is in court by himself. He looks for his mother but she didn't show up. He wants to believe that she has a good reason for not being there but the truth is, she was out with her girls the night before and she just couldn't make it out of bed in time for the trial.

Everybody in the court room stands as the judge comes in, the prosecutor makes her opening arguments and the court appointed defense councilor takes a look at his file and gives up without any argument.

"The defendant will stand" the judge orders and Gerrard rises to his feet, "You have been found guilty of driving a stolen car, attempting to elude the police and resisting arrest. For your crimes, you have been sentenced to 10 years in the Alabama Penial System. You will spend the next 4 years in juvenile detention until your 18th birthday at which time you will be transferred to Alabama State Corrections where you will serve the rest of your sentence."

◆   ◆   ◆

The gavel slams down; the guard grabs Gerrard by the arm and takes him out of the courtroom to a waiting cell for transport to the Juvenile Detention Center.

4 years have passed in the blink of an eye, Gerrard is now 18 and it is moving day.

The bus pulls up; "Alabama Corrections" is on the side of it. Gerrard gets on and walks towards the back of the bus. "Hey sweet thang, look at that booty, you gone be mine tonight" he hears from some of prisoners as he walks by. He takes a seat, in the back, by himself and the bus pulls out of the loading area on to the road. The ride to the prison is a long one and it gives Gerrard time to think about everything that has lead up to this point. He thinks about going with his brother to rob that diner, he thinks about hiding in the car while the police and fire units swarmed the diner and how he never saw his brother alive again, he thinks about the police chase in the stolen car that made him spend the last 4 years in Juvenile Detention, he thinks about his mother…. the mother that couldn't take the time to visit her youngest son in the detention center, he thinks about everything that got him to this point.

The bus arrives at the prison and the inmates are ushered off. They are taken to intake where they are given the welcome to prison speech by the Chief of the guards, issued their bedding and separated into groups. Each group goes to a different block and each one of the group's members goes to a different cell. Gerrard gets one all by himself, they all do but it affects him the most. It starts to sink in that this is his life now and it is not a good feeling. It's late and there is just enough time to make the bed before the door slams shut, then lights out. It gets pretty quiet at night, so quiet that everybody can hear you cry.

The next day starts and Gerrard is in the big leagues. For the 4 years that he was in Juvenile Detention, Gerrard was the HTIC (Head Thug in Charge) but now, now he's the new bitch on the on the block…or so they think.

. . .

It is lunchtime in the correction center, all the inmates are in the cafeteria and Gerrard is walking to a table with his tray of food when he gets tripped, spilling his food and falling to his knees.

"Yeah lil bitch, stay just like that", one of the inmates is standing in front of Gerrard and has plans to make him his bitch but that's not going to work for Gerrard. He takes his tray and shoves into the inmate's groin, when the inmate doubles over in pain Gerrard grabs the back of his neck and with one swift move stands and brings his knee into the inmate's face, breaking his nose. The inmate falls to the floor, screaming in pain and blood gushing from his broken nose. Gerrard stands over him, raises his foot and starts stomping the inmates face. As Gerrard is beating this man to within an inch of his life, he begins to feel something, something that he likes. He feels powerful, he feels in control, he feels like this is who he was meant to be. The guards fight their way through the crowd, grab Gerrard and slam him to the floor as they hand cuff him and shackle his feet. Gerrard looks over at the man he just beat into unconsciousness and smiles. The guards lift him up and carry him out of the cafeteria. They take him to solitary confinement unshackle him and release his hands. They leave him without restraints but still covered in the other man's blood, then slam the door as they exit the cell. Now, in solitaire confinement, Gerrard has time to think about what just happened…he liked beating that man and can't wait to do it again.

It has been a learning experience and after four years with time off for good behavior his time at the State Pen is done. The last years were relatively uneventful, in comparison to the first day but still an education. While he was in prison he found out that his mother died and everything that she owned was turned over to the state, so there was nothing for him to go home to. He found out that she had died through a letter sent to him by the man that is going be his Parole Officer. The day he leaves the facility, Gerrard uses the bus ticket that was provided by the state and gets on the Grey Hound headed for Birmingham. As he rides, he reflects on everything that has happened to him since that night and he comes to the conclusion that everything that has happened to him is the fault of his brother, but since his brother is dead, there is no way to resolve his anger issues.

Once he is back in the "Ham", Gerrard makes it to his old neighborhood.

"Gerrard?" a voice from his past calls out, "Gerrard is that you?" it's his old junior high friend Darryl or Dee. "Yeah man it's me." Gerrard responds. The two talk about the old days and Dee tells Gerrard that he was sorry about his mom but that if he needs a place to stay he can live with him until he got back on his feet. Gerrard takes him up on his offer and when the two get back to Dee's apartment, Gerrard sees how Dee is living and he wants to know what he has to do to get what his old friend has.

"If you want to get all of this, I'ma introduce you to my boy and he will hook you up." When Gerrard meets Dee's boy, they talk and he sets Gerrard up to become one of the most dangerous drug dealers in Birmingham. In less than six months Gerrard is running the Eastside of town. He has his hands in everything from drugs to human trafficking and prostitution. There is nothing on, the Eastside of town that goes down that he doesn't know about, so when he heard about the social worker that was once a police officer, the police officer that killed his brother, was trying to bring an end to his reign, he had to get his revenge.

Gerrard switched his anger from his brother to Ken and that wasn't good for Ken. All he could think about was getting back at the mutha fucka and making him pay for all the shit that he had been trough but, he needed a plan. So, when his boys came back and told him about the block party that the neighborhood was having and how Ken and the men from the neighborhood jacked them up when they tried to shut it down and how Ken was there with Niecy and her little girl, it gave him an idea. Gerrard comes up with a plan and it wouldn't be long before he set it into motion.

Chapter Eight

NEW BUSINESS

Ken is at work, and it is the end of an unusually stressful day. He is done with his interviews and ready for a night of cigars, whiskey and smooth jazz. He is about to head out of the office building when his phone rings. It's Neicey's so he answers, "Hey you."

Niecy responds, "Hey Smiley, me and baby girl want to invite you over to dinner tonight to thank you for helping us turn the neighborhood around?" Ken is pleased to hear her sounding so well and since his plans are pretty much something that he can do any night, he is more than happy to join the two ladies for dinner. "Sure, I would love to have dinner with you and the kiddo, what time should I be there?"

Neicey responds with a high level of excitement in her voice, "Great! Um, be here around 7 o'clock, were having salad and pot roast." she tells him, and he asks if he can bring anything. She says that they have everything they need and that all he needs to do is show up. Ken acknowledges what she said but tells her that he will stop and get the soda that he knows that baby girl likes. Neicey says ok and they hang up.

It's been three weeks since the night of the block party and it's hard to believe just how much the neighborhood is beginning to look like its old self. People are out walking around and talking with friends, kids are running up and down the sidewalks and having the time of their lives. The general atmosphere is one of peace and prosperity. The old neighborhood has really started to make a change for the better and Ken is rather pleased with its renaissance and with himself but mostly with the neighborhood. With all the changes that have been taking place, it is hard to imagine that G is gone but it's been awhile since anyone has heard from him or his boys and it looks like he has disappeared, but Ken knows he is still there somewhere and he knows it won't be long before he makes his presence known.

Ken stops at the corner grocery store to get the soda for baby girl. When he walks in, he is greeted by the strangely dressed and slightly confused looking clerk,

"Hey man, how you doin tonight can we help you?" The clerk asks. Ken looks at him in a slightly confused, highly amused way.

Ken tells him, "Naw, I'm just getting a soda." The clerk nods and laughs then tells Ken the sodas are on isle two, Ken thanks him and heads in that direction. Just as Ken grabs the soda from the shelf, his phone rings, it's Neicey.

"Hey what's up? I am getting the soda now and I will be headed that way soon." There is nothing but silence. "Hello?" Ken asks again, still nothing.

Then a male voice comes over the phone, "Yeah mutha fucka, I got yo bitch, what you gone do now?" Ken stops in his tracks; he knows it's G but something deep in his gut is praying that it's not. Still he asks the question, "Who is this and where is Neicey?" Again a brief silence before the man speaks.

"This G bitch and I got these two hoes and gone do what the fuck I want with them, now what the fuck you gone do bout dat shit bitch?" before Ken gets a chance to answer or ask more questions, G hangs up the phone.

Ken stands there for a minute in disbelief and thinks, *No this punk ass bitch didn't just go after Neicey and baby girl, no the fuck he didn't.* Ken puts the soda back on the shelf and starts walking out of the store. The clerk asks if everything is ok, Ken says to him "I don't know yet." as he walks out of the door. Once outside Ken gets in his truck and speeds out of the parking lot headed toward Neicey's apartment.

It takes him 5 minutes to get to Neicey's apartment building. As he makes his way up the stairs, all kinds of scenarios of what he could find run through his head. When he gets there, he finds the door kicked in, the lights still on and signs of a struggle everywhere. Ken calls out to the two ladies, "Neicey, Baby girl!" no response. Ken walks through the door and goes room to room, looking for something that he hopes he won't find. Thankfully, the search turns up nothing. He looks at the shape of the apartment and it pisses him off, even more than when G called and said he had the women and was going to do what he wanted to them. All he did was try to help an old friend and he, he tried to do it the right way but this fool won't let him do it like that. No, this young, stupid fool wants him to be Smiley again. Well, if that's what he wants, that's what he is going to get. Before Ken leaves Neicey's apartment he calls Sonja. When she answers, "Matthews, what do you want?", not her warmest greeting but not the coldest one either,

She stops just long enough for him to say, "You are the last person that I wanted to bother tonight but I couldn't think of who else to call...I need your help."

Sonja is silent for a minute but only for a minute, then "What's up?" her entire domineer changes, maybe because she hears the desperation in his voice or maybe because...doesn't matter, she is willing to help.

"This lil punk ass..." Ken stops himself from going into a rage, "G... G took both of them, Neicey and Baby Girl. I need for you send some officers over here to secure the scene. Will you do that for me?" he asks her. She says nothing at first but then she responds, "Where is Neicey's apartment?" she asks. Ken tells her the address and they end the call.

Ken is still in a bit of shock, but his old patrol training is starting to kick in. He leaves the apartment and makes his way outside to wait for the police, as he goes down the stairs, he makes another phone call to the one person that he knows cares about the two ladies just as much as he does, "Uncle Tommy, he has both of them. Can you do what I pray you can do?" Uncle tommy answers, "You tell me where." The two men talk until the police arrive on the scene. Ken shows them Neicey's apartment, they take control of the area and Ken backs away but keeps a vigilant eye on everything that is happening, waiting for a clue to find Niecy and Baby Girl.

◆　　◆　　◆

G and his boys have Neicey and Baby Girl on the other side of town, in a dark and abandoned warehouse, locked up in what was the tool locker back when the warehouse made steel beams for the construction of buildings and tracks for the railroads. As Neicey tries to comfort her daughter she fights back the fear that is building up inside of her own gut.

One of G's boys decides that they don't look scared enough, "Yeah bitch, I see you scared, ain't nobody gone save yo asses?" he screams at the two hostages.

G and his right hand man Dee, are sitting in what used to be the shop manager's office, they're going over the plan to take back the neighborhood, "We keep these two bitches and tell ole boy that he better get his ass out the neighborhood and take the police with him, so we can take that bitch back." Dee tells G, but G doesn't hear him. His mind is on his next move, selling drugs and robbing people are easy compared to kidnapping and now that he has made the jump from street thug to hostage taker, he realizes that he can't let them go. The only thing that breaks his concentration is the sound of one of his boys screaming at his hostages.

G screams at his boy, "Hey! Shut the fuck up. I'm trying to think." The warehouse gets quiet except for the sobbing sounds of a small child and the mother that is trying to comfort her.

The sound of Baby Girl crying infuriates G more and before anyone can react, G is out of the office, down the stairs, and at the opening to the tool locker.

"Ho didn't I tell you to keep that little bitch quite, I ought to shoot both y'all asses now and be done with it." He pulls out his gun to shoot them but stops himself before he does the deed. He's not sure about any of this anymore, he just wants it to be over and he only sees one way of that happening.

"Bitch, I should put a bullet in yo ass. Yo brought that mutha fucka back, you why all my shit is fucked up. You…", G stops talking. Neicey has this look in her eyes. A look that burns G to his soul, then she tells him,

"You can't do shit to me that ain't already been done. I hoed these streets, I have smoked more shit than I ever want to remember, I have almost died more times than any one person ever should and you think I'm afraid of you?"

G has no response for her defiance, so he slaps her across her face and knocks her to the floor, "Bitch I own you!" Neicey looks up at G from the floor, wipes the blood from her mouth and remains as defiant as any woman whose child is being held by sociopath can be.

Then, bang! G shoots her, once in the in the stomach. Baby Girl screams out in horror, she has just watched her mother be shot by this monster and there was nothing she could've done to stop it.

G, in shock himself at what he has just done, screams an order to his boys, "Fuck this bitch, leave her ass there to rot, let's go." as he drags Baby Girl away from her mother and out of the warehouse, as she is crying and screaming, "Mommy, mommy!" G not only shocked himself and Baby Girl with this act, he scared all of his boys. Now, the last thing they want to do is piss him off as they all follow behind him, out of the warehouse.

•   •   •

Once Sonja arrives at Neicey's apartment after she reads Ken the riot, he gets out of the way and lets them work. As he stands there, observing everything, he notices a smudge in the carpet. He takes a closer look and then calls for an evidence tech. The evidence tech takes a sample and tells Ken that it looks like a mixture of oil and old metal shavings, then it hits Ken like a ton of bricks, *The steel mills!*

Ken knows where they are, but he doesn't want to let the officers know that he knows where they are, he doesn't want to take a chance on Neicey and Baby Girl being caught up in a cross fire, besides, he has already called his back up. Ken ask the evidence techs if they have the scene and tells Sonja he is going home but will be by his phone if they find anything.

Ken is headed down the stairs and to his truck, when Sonja catches up to him, "Matthews, we need to talk about this." Ken turns and looks at her, "Can this wait until later? I really need to get some rest and I really am not up for you fussing at me tonight." She just looks at him as he turns around and goes to his truck.

As soon as he gets in his truck and pulls off, he makes a phone call to Uncle Tommy, "I know where they are, meet me at the corner of Georgia Rd and Oporto, there is a water tower there, makes a good spot for those specific skills of yours." Uncle Tommy agrees and hangs up. Ken increases his speed and heads to the old steel mill.

Even at high speed, it's 20 minutes before Ken can get across town to the old steel mill. When he arrives, he parks the truck about 500 feet away from the warehouse, draws his gun from the glove compartment and starts his quick but tactical approach to the warehouse, checking the water tower for Uncle Tommy. Once at the mill, he checks the water tower one more time with the hope that Uncle Tommy is there. Only seconds pass before Ken decides to go in. He scans the main entrance before he moves into the room. Sticking close to the wall, he makes his way through the main entrance to milling room. He takes the entrance to the milling room with the speed and tact that he that he took front door. His gun up and ready to shoot anything or anyone that pops up. As soon as he enters the room, Ken hears a faint whimpering and begins to move in that direction. The closer he gets, the louder the whimpering gets until there is no mistaking what it is. On the floor, about 10 feet in front of him, Neicey is laying, with her hands pressed to her stomach, bleeding out. Ken runs to her side and places his hand on hers. He grabs his phone and calls 911, "I need the paramedics at the mill on Georgia and Oporto!" after a he tells them what he needs them for, the dispatcher tells him that they are on their way. Ken hangs up with 911 and calls Uncle Tommy. "They shot her, get down here A.S.A.P, I need you on my back while we wait for the paramedics." Uncle Tommy comes down from the tower and is on his way to Ken and Neicey. While Ken is waiting on Uncle Tommy, Neicey starts to speak. "They took her Smiley. They took my baby girl. Don't let them hurt her, don't let her get hurt."

Ken tries to comfort Neicey, "Shh rest, the paramedics are on their way." Ken tries to comfort her but she is too worried about her daughter and Ken is worried about the blood she is losing.

What seems like an eternity but is actually only a few seconds pass as Uncle Tommy makes it to Ken and Neicey. When he gets there, Ken is kneeling and holding Niecey as she fades in and out of consciousness. Far off in the background, Ken can hear the sirens from the police and ambulance getting closer. As Uncle Tommy gets to them, Ken tells him to take over. "I'm going get Baby Girl." the two men nod to each other as Ken lets Uncle Tommy take over.

"You get that mother fucker and bring my baby girl home safe!" Uncle Tommy screams at Ken as he runs out of the mill headed to his truck. Ken gets in his truck and sequels the tires as he pulls out on to the road...It's time to end this.

Chapter Nine

THIS IS THE END

Ken is driving through the city trying to anticipate where G and his boys are taking Baby Girl. He can't get the thought that Neicey could die out of his head but he is about to take on G and all his boys, alone, and he needs all of his energy centered.

I have focus; I can't go up against 'G' worrying about Neicey.. Ken finally gets his head in the game when his phone rings. It's Neicey's phone number on the caller ID.

"Where are you?" Ken is straight to the point when he answers his phone, prompting G's response. "Yeah mutha fucka, we gone settle this shit now. Meet me at 1st and 52nd, no cops and remember…I got the little girl." G hangs up and Ken makes a U-turn in the middle street. In no time Ken is headed towards 1st and 52nd, with every intention of ending this tonight.

While driving, Ken develops a plan to take on G and his boys. He knows it won't be a fair fight and it's not because he is outnumbered, it's because he has the advantage. When Ken was a patrol officer this was his beat and he knows it like the back of his hand. He remembers the lay out of the building at the corner of 1st and 52nd and he knows the best way to approach it without being seen.

While en route, Ken's phone rings. He looks at the caller ID and thinks, *Damn.* this is not going to be a call that he wants to take, so he is hesitant to answer it but… "Hello Lieutenant." Sonja is not in the best of moods. After she heard about Neicey, she figured out that he is going after G and Baby Girl.

"Matthews, what the hell are you doing? Have you lost your damn mind?" Clearly these are all rhetorical questions, but Ken tries to lighten the moment…it's not going to work, but he tries it anyway.

"So to what do I owe the pleasure of your call?" She is not amused, and he can sense it. Through her silence, she speaks volumes, but Ken knows that there is no other way to fix this, so he tells her, "I have to finish this, he has baby girl, he wants me, and I have to end this."

She knows Ken and what he is capable of and that scares her. "Ken, where are you?"

He can hear her whole demeanor change, "I'm where I need to be." then he hangs up the phone. He couldn't take the chance that she would send a police unit to stop him, nor could he take the chance that an approaching patrol car would spook G. No matter what the cost, he had to keep Baby Girl safe and that meant he had to do this alone.

•   •   •

Ken is on 1st Ave getting close to 1st and 52nd. He parks his truck three blocks away from location, gets out, grabs his service weapon and his collapsible baton out of the glove compartment then starts the slow tactical approach to the building. A long time ago 1st and 52nd was the club to go to, it would have live music on Saturday nights and brunch on the first Sunday of the month but now it is just an old abandoned building that is in need of tearing down and tonight, tonight it is going to be where this unfinished business gets finished. Ken gets a block away and stops. He is just close enough to see two of G's boys guarding the entrance, *that's two*, he thinks to himself. Just then, another one of G's boys comes from around the side of the building, *that's three, I can take three*, he says to himself.

Ken starts to move closer then another one of G's boys comes from around the other side of the building… *I can take four, God please help me take four?* he prays as he gets closer. Then the two that walked up, turn around and go back to where they came from. Then, like a miracle from the heavens, one of the two guys that were in the front says something to the other guy then goes inside the building.

"Thank you" Ken says quickly as he begins his approach to the building. He moves to take the first guy from behind. In less than a heartbeat, Ken puts his foot in the bend of the guys' knee breaking his stance, then wraps his arm around the guys' neck cutting off his air and the blood flow to his brain, in seconds the guy is out. Ken drags his unconscious body to a nearby dumpster and tosses him. Just then, the door opens and its other guy coming back outside. Ken rushes him putting his forearm in his throat and slamming him into the brick wall, knocking him out instantly. Ken just lets his limb body fall to the ground, then makes his way to guy number three. As he gets closer to the third guy, Ken pulls out his old collapsible baton. When he is in striking distance, Ken whispers "hey" extends the baton and as the guy turns around, Ken strikes him across the jaw with the baton in an uppercut motion causing his head to snap back with enough force to knock him out, one more, then on to G. Ken makes quick work of the last guy using the same skills that he used on the third and now he enters the building with the same tactical entry that he used when he was an officer. Sticking close to the wall he makes his way around the room, to an opening that he hopes will lead to G and Baby Girl. When Ken gets to the door and looks in, he sees G, Baby Girl and Dee.

Ken takes a step back into the darkness and uses his baton to make a noise. G and Dee are startled by the noise and G tells Dee to go check it out. Dee disappears into the darkness, "Uummff, thud" is all G hears. "Dee!" G cries out but there is no response. G gets scared and grabs Baby Girl, then calls out to his boy again, "Dee!"

Ken answers, "Dee can't help you now, it's just me and you" Ken steps through the door way and into the light, Baby Girl screams "Smiley!" and G, with his arm around her neck, tells her "Shut up bitch." Ken answers him for her, "Mutha fucka, you don't talk to her like that."

The two men find themselves in the middle of a scene from an old west movie, both men have their guns aimed at the other. It is at this point that G decides that he needs some questions answered. "Is this how you shot my brother that night? I saw them take you out on a stretcher and my brother out in a body bag. Why did you kill my brother?"

Ken is stunned for a second but only a second, "You were there that night? I didn't see you." Ken begins to question everything he remembers about that night.

"Yeah I was there, I was in the car when you pulled up, I heard the shots, I saw the other cops come rushing to you and I saw my brother leave in a body bag. Yeah, I was there." G's voice trembles as he recounts what he saw that night, as if he was that teenage boy again.

Ken can understand how that teenage boy would've felt but this ain't that boy, this is the man that has kept the people in the neighborhood, Ken's old beat, terrorized for the last two years. This is the man that shot Neicey. This is the man that took Baby Girl hostage, and this is the man that Ken has to take down, preferably alive but at this point, dead will do. Ken has G locked in his sights, as he is slowly squeezing the trigger, a little voice speaks out. "Smiley, don't kill him." It takes Ken a minute to realize that the little voice is not in his head. It's Baby Girl, the reason why he is here.

Ken releases the trigger and speaks, "If you put your gun down and let her go, we can work this out." Ken tries to reason with G but it is not working.

"Work it out? Da fuck you mean work it out?" G is not going for the idea of this ending peacefully and he grips his gun tighter as his hand starts to shake. "I ain't going back to jail, either you going to kill me or you gone let me go but I ain't putting my gun down." That's not what Ken wanted to hear, and he now knows this is not going to end the way he hoped.

Ken squares his aim and starts his slow steady squeeze again, "This is your last chance. You don't want it to end like this, not like your brother." These words are Ken's last plea with G and they strike a nerve.

"My brother? Fuck you!" BANG! Two shots fired at the same time, one 9mm and one .45. Seconds go by and G loosens his grip on Baby Girl. He drops his gun and falls to the floor. Baby Girl runs to Ken, grabs on to his leg and holds on for dear life, "You ok Baby Girl?" Ken asks her, she looks up at him and nods her head yes. G is lying on the floor, bleeding and in pain but alive, Ken points to a chair and tells Baby Girl, "Go sit over there... I'm going to go check on him and then I am going to take you to see your momma, ok?" Baby girl nods her head again and then goes to sit down. Ken cautiously walks over to G, kicks the gun out of his way and then kneels next to G.

"You shot me! You should've killed me!" G screams at Ken, "Yeah, I should've, maybe next time but tonight we both get to live." Ken shot G in his right shoulder about an inch from his cerotic artery. A disabling shot but not a fatal one, provided he can get medical attention as soon as possible. Ken pulls out his phone and dials 911. Ken tells the operator where he is, that G has been shot and how bad the wound is and about all of G's boys, hopefully still unconscious, and where they are located. The operator confirms the information and tells Ken that the police and the paramedics are on the way. His next call is to Sonja.

When she answers the call, she tears into Ken, "Where the hell are you?" is her first question "Are you ok?" is her second. Ken is not surprised by her question but he did just shoot a man after taking on his small army so it took him a little time before he answered. "I'm at 1st and 52nd, Baby Girl is safe, the Police and Medics are on the way, and I'm ok." She doesn't say a word but Ken can imagine how mad she must be. "I just wanted to let you know that I am still alive and everything is under control…now." She still doesn't say a word, but Ken keeps his phone to his ear.

After a few intense seconds, she finally speaks, "You are not a police officer anymore. You cannot take these types of matters into your own hands…I'm glad that you are ok." The last thing that she says throws him off a bit, but he likes that she is concerned about him.

"Ok, I will talk to you later." then he hangs up. Ken can hear sirens in the background, getting louder as they get closer. Baby Girl comes over to him and he picks her up, "You ok kiddo?" he asks her, and she smiles and nods her head yes. G is lying there in pain as the police and paramedics make it through the door and into the room. The paramedics rush to G and the police go to Ken and Baby Girl. Ken hands her over to the first officer that gets to him and surrenders his gun to the next, together they walk out of the room. As they walk out of the building the sun is starting to come up and the weather is feeling great. For the first time, in a long time, Ken is looking forward to putting that night and everything that has happened behind him.

◆   ◆   ◆

Several weeks pass and the morning that Ken saved Baby Girl from G is all but a memory. Everything is back to normal in the neighborhood and things are looking up. It's now early fall and Baby Girl is excited about starting school. It will be her first time and since she tested so well on the placement exam, she is able to skip Pre-K and is going straight to Kindergarten. Neicey survived that night and while her surgery was rough, she made it through like a trooper and now she is making substantial progress with her physical therapy and the neighborhood is getting ready for her to come home. Ken received a reprimand and is still on suspension from work. It's without pay, but Ken has a substantial savings account, so it's more like a vacation. Sonja went off on him like she was still his patrol sergeant but later they made up, most of the night and the next morning but then she got mad at him again. Everything seemed to be coming up roses for everyone, everyone that is except for G. He was arrested, then transported to the hospital where the doctors performed surgery to remove the bullet from his shoulder. Then he was placed under 24-hour guard until he was transported to the county jail. Once at the jail, he was placed in isolation and put on suicide watch while he awaited trail. He was charged with kidnapping for taking Baby Girl and Neicey hostage, felony assault for shooting Neicey and criminal trespassing for being on the property at 1st and 52nd. It seems that even though the club had closed down and the building was empty, the woman that owned the club still owns the building and she hadn't given anyone, including G, permission to use it.

•   •   •

G is sitting in isolation, thinking about everything that went wrong with his life, when the guard bangs on the door, "You have a visitor."

G rises from the bed and walks over to the door, "Visitor?" G asks. The door opens and G walks out. He is handcuffed and shackled per procedure for anyone that is on suicide watch, then lead to the visitor's room. He was not expecting a visitor, especially this one. G walks over to the table where Ken is sitting but remains standing.

"Man, what the fuck do you want?" he asks Ken. "Just sit down." Ken tells him.

The two men just stare at each other, then Ken speaks again, with a calmness in his voice that is supposed to ease the tension between them, "Man just sit down so we can talk, man to man, eye to eye."

G sits down, and Ken starts, "Listen, I know that right now it seems like I am the reason that you have gone through everything that you have been through and for that, I do apologize. No one should have to deal with what you have had to deal with…" G looks at Ken with a small glimmer of hope in his eyes, "but, in all honesty, this was your choice." and just like that, the glimmer of hope is gone but Ken continues.

"You went with your brother that night and when you got out of juvenile detention, you came back to your old neighborhood and became the biggest problem that it ever had. This is your doing but I want to help you get past this and help you become the man that you want to be."

G looks at Ken, then speaks. "You want to help me? Are you for real?" he asks Ken with a look of disbelief on his face, "Man you the reason why I'm in here. You killed my brother. You messed up my business. You shot me!" G screams, and Ken tries to calm him down, but he's not having any of that. G stands up, pushing his chair back, "Man get the fuck out of here, go find somebody else to run yo game on. Guard! Take me back to my cell."

G turns around and walks away, leaving Ken sitting at the table. Ken leans back in his chair and watches as the guard grabs G's arm and escorts him out of the meeting room. Ken knows that the only way he could help G is if G wanted his help and clearly he doesn't. Ken gets up from his seat, realizing that there is nothing he can do to help this young man and walks out of the meeting room. Once outside, he takes a deep breath of the fresh air begins to walk towards his truck.

Ken can't help but feel partially responsible for everything this young man has been through, but the truth is we all have to face the consequences of the choices we make. Still, he can't help but think to himself, "If I had checked that empty car first that night, maybe he wouldn't have turned out the way that he has. Maybe if I hadn't had to kill his brother. Maybe if…." Ken realizes that all the maybes in the world can't change what has happened. He is also reminded of the harsh reality that no matter how much he wants to; he can't help everyone but that as long as one of the ones that he is trying help gets what they need…it's a good day.

Ken pulls a cigar from his coat pocket, lights it and walks towards his truck. As he gets to where it is parked, his phone rings. He pulls it out of his pocket, takes a look at the caller ID. It is a number that he doesn't recognize but he answers it anyway. "Hello" his generic but inquisitive greeting. "Sargent Matthews, long time no hear."

Ken is stunned for a second, he is having a hard time believing his ears. This is a blast from his past. Not because he hasn't been called Sargent Matthews in twenty plus years but because of who it is on the other end, "Gunner James? I had heard you were dead?" Ken says to the man on the other end.

"No not yet. How have you been? That's good to hear, listen, I need your help. My granddaughter is missing, and I remember how good you are at tracking people. How soon can you make it to New Orleans?"

Gunner James was always straight to the point and if he is asking for Ken's help, after all these years, it has got to be something that no one else can help him with.

"Gunner, last time you and I worked together, if I remember correctly, we were mistaken for terrorist." The Gunner chuckles and Ken continues, "but if you need me, you know I'm there." The Gunner responds, "I knew that I could count on you…thanks." then he hangs up the phone.

Ken starts making plans to go to New Orleans and tries to figure out a good excuse to take off work, especially since he is still on suspension. Ken makes a call," Hey boss, I know that I am still on suspension for the next few days but a family emergency just came up and I need to take some time off…..."

CPSIA information can be obtained
at www.ICGtesting.com
Printed in the USA
LVHW041752190523
747519LV00019B/134